The Halloween Misfits Conference

Held at the Famous Clown Motel

Meg Infiorati Fleming

Dedication

For my mother, who read everything I ever wrote.

Acknowledgment

I started this story years ago; through several iterations with friends at the Brooksville Writers Club (Brooksville, FL), I finally finished. Special thanks go to Alicia and Chris. Your insights were invaluable.

I also want to thank my project coordinator, Martin, and the rest of the team at KDP. Who knows if I will publish another story, but you made the process easy.

Finally, thank you Vijay Mehar, owner of the historic Clown Motel in Tonopah, NV, and his very talented CEO and art director, Hame Anand for giving me free rein on content while using their wonderful hotel as the story backdrop.

Contents

Dedication.. iii

Acknowledgment iv

BOOK 1 DANNY 1

Chapter 1 Time For Halloween Plans.....................2

Chapter 2 The Clown Motel 6

Chapter 3 Let The Fun Begin.........................11

Chapter 4 A Delicious Lunch 17

Chapter 5 Good Friends 31

Chapter 6 Graveyard 35

Chapter 7 The Tour 51

Chapter 8 The Kitchen 58

BOOK TWO ALISON 66

Chapter 1 Breakfast.................................67

Chapter 2 Alone 76

Chapter 3 No Nick 87

Chapter 4 Party Time 90

Chapter 5 96

Chapter 6 Homeward Bound 100

Epilogue 102

About The Author 106

BOOK 1
DANNY

Chapter 1
Time For Halloween Plans

"Danny, DANNY!" she cried with delight. "The invitation is here!"

"Hold your cackling, I can't hear you," I said, coming into the kitchen. "What's all the fuss?"

"Oh, it's here, it's HERE! The invitation to the Halloween Misfits Conference—and FINALLY, there's a special track just for rodeo clowns! Can you believe it? Isn't that just the most wonderful news?" Alison was nearly in tears as she ran to hug me.

I took the paper from her and read the invitation, blinking in disbelief. There had never been a special track for rodeo clowns. Ever. We just didn't fit. We weren't scary like Dracula or your average wicked witch, and we weren't exactly in the same league as your friendly neighborhood ghost either.

Clowns were... well, creepy—if you took a poll. Most of us blame that on movies and books. Stephen King, the famous writer that he is, made his fortune turning the most mundane things terrifying—high school girls, dogs and other pets, cars, hotel rooms, even fog. But his book *IT*? That made history for clowns. And not in a good way. According to *Smithsonian Magazine*, it's considered the beginning of the end for us.

Topping it all off was the crackpot field of psychology that actually came up with a term for the fear of clowns: *coulrophobia*. They even added it to their official list of specific phobias. For goodness' sake, I thought, clowns are just people in work costumes—no different than a businessperson in a suit or a McDonald's employee in their standard uniform. (Sans Ronald McDonald, of course—which, by the way, is still a huge loss deeply felt in the clown world.)

After all, the Ronald McDonald character has raised millions for charity since he burst onto the scene in 1974. And yet, have you seen him in a TV commercial lately? Didn't think so. Another relic lost to time. Oh well. Some things I just can't fix—or even bother to fret over. And this is one of them.

What I *could* do, I figured, was share in my wife's excitement about the upcoming Halloween Misfits Weekend, scheduled for October 27th and 28th. It didn't exactly thrill me, but it was her once-a-year tradition she insisted she was doing "for me." And I'll admit, this year's location was at least interesting: the world-famous Clown Motel in Tonopah, Nevada. The owner is a genuine clown lover and has over 1,000 clown dolls and artifacts on display.

"Well, Alison," I said, "guess you'd better hop on Kayak and find us a flight—unless you'd rather drive? It's only about eight hours. We could hit Vegas for the night and catch a show first, then drive up to the motel. Your call. I'll jump online and reserve our room."

Chapter 2
The Clown Motel

Alison had been chattering almost nonstop for the entire three hours since we left Vegas—but I didn't mind.

"I'm so glad we stayed in Las Vegas yesterday," she said, then sighed wistfully. "It felt like our honeymoon again, being in that fancy hotel last night."

Snapping out of the memory, she added, "I really am excited to see the Clown Motel, but my goodness—it's surely a long way from anywhere!"

She wasn't wrong. We'd been passing signs for the motel for nearly an hour now, and it felt like we'd never actually get there. So, we just settled in for the ride, cruising through the fall desert and passing dusty little wannabe ghost towns along the way. Each one had the usual—one or two stores, maybe a restaurant, a gas station—but the people we saw looked haggard and worn. I suppose living out here in this wild wasteland might leave you a little sunbaked, inside and out.

Finally, up ahead, there it was—the sign we'd been waiting for.

15 MILES TO THE WORLD-FAMOUS CLOWN MOTEL

It loomed over the road, the biggest sign you could imagine. There was a cartoon of the Clown Motel, complete with a cheerful puppet clown dancing beside it—2.5 Miles Ahead. It proudly announced that all rooms were air-conditioned and that Wi-Fi was free for guests.

We sailed past the Tonopah service road exit, continuing a couple more miles until we reached the motel, which didn't so much have an exit as a simple left turn straight off the highway and into the gravel parking lot.

"Well, that surely looks inviting," said Alison, echoing exactly what I was thinking. It was well past lunchtime, and I was both hungry and parched.

#

I'm a rodeo clown. And while most of my peers wouldn't be caught dead at the annual clown get-together, Alison and I enjoyed the camaraderie of like-minded people.

Most rodeo clowns are really stuntmen in disguise. They don't mind taking a few hits on the weekend to clear an extra $75K a year. It's a second job for many—insurance agents, bookkeepers, mechanics by day; adrenaline junkies in makeup by night. But Alison and I were in a good place financially, so this was my only job.

With no kids, rodeos nearly every weekend, and steady bookings, I was earning a higher-than-average salary. Alison worked as an online U.S. history professor for the local university, so she could teach from anywhere. Sometimes she came with me on the road; other times she stayed home.

We had a life that felt pretty close to free. Our small house in Phoenix and our motorhome were both paid off. We'd boosted our retirement savings by thousands just from traveling in the RV alone—cutting down on hotel costs and eating like kings on the rodeo circuit's dime.

But this weekend was going to be different.

Alison was on vacation, and she assured me we were going to thoroughly enjoy the amenities of the motel and the activities planned for the Halloween Misfits event. There wasn't much information about the special clown track—but I figured it probably included a couple of seminars on clowning tricks, some new gags or props making the rounds, and, of course, the usual Halloween Scarefest Party.

For anyone arriving on the 30th, there was also a nighttime tour of the town cemetery after the buffet dinner, complete with ghost stories about the miners who once lived—and died—in Tonopah. That included the infamous Tonopah-Belmont Mine Fire of 1911.

Chapter 3
Let The Fun Begin

We pulled into the parking lot and saw it was only half full—for now. I knew it would be packed by the end of the day. With only 31 rooms available, I was glad we'd made our reservation early and picked our room.

Many of the attendees had to settle for one of the six other hotels in Tonopah—and that was something I hated. I couldn't stand driving to and from events. And don't even get me started on shuttle buses. Just the thought of one made me flash back to those bumpy, noisy elementary school days.

The Clown Motel was something of a museum. Most of its 31 rooms were decked out in themes based on clown characters from TV or movies. A few had more subtle décor, with just a touch of clown here or there—but the common areas were unmistakably on-brand. The lobby, restaurant, gift shop, and hallways were filled with familiar clown memorabilia, recognizable to anyone who'd grown up with even a sliver of pop culture.

I'd booked us a simple clown suite—no horror themes, thanks. I had no interest in staying in one of the rooms modeled after famous creepy clowns. That was more the style of the die-hard horror fans attending this event.

Rodeo clowns? We were a different breed entirely. We were working clowns. And by working, I mean the job could be downright dangerous.

Some clowns entertain—or get swarmed by—packs of tiny, shrieking tots. Others get chased by kids who think it's funny to "get" the clown because they saw something scary in a movie. But that wasn't our audience.

We dodged ambushes from creatures the size of compact SUVs—creatures with razor-sharp horns and zero patience. We coaxed stubborn bulls into chutes they didn't want to be in. Trickier still was drawing their attention away when a cowboy—or cowgirl—was down and needed rescuing. A bucking, two-thousand-pound hunk of raw muscle charging your way isn't something you forget. It's not just dangerous. It's madness. It's what we did. And I loved it.

But this weekend? I was off-duty. The only dodging I planned to do was at the dessert table—and I already knew I'd probably lose that battle.

"Okay, Alison, let's get checked in and grab some lunch," I said.

Alison looked around thoughtfully. "We'll probably have to eat at the hotel or head back to that last exit into town," she said.

"It's up to you, Allison; either is fine with me, lunch is my top priority," I said.

"Well, this is surely a clown's happy place," Alison said, her eyes wide with delight. "Look at all the wonderful memorabilia! And Danny—there's a gift shop too! And all the workers! They're dressed like famous clowns! I can't imagine having to clean or make up beds in those costumes, but I guess that's all part of the fun for the guests."

"Good afternoon, Mr. Harrison," said the desk clerk as we approached the front desk.

He looked exactly like Bozo the Clown—an uncanny likeness, really. If there was ever a true American icon in the clown world, it was Bozo, straight out of the 1950s—and now here he was, staring right at me.

"Uh, yes, that's right," I said, caught a bit off guard. "I'm Daniel Harrison, and this is my wife, Alison."

Something about Bozo knowing my name unsettled me. I hadn't even thought about Bozo in nearly fifty years—not since the summer I turned eight. Most of my friends back then thought the show was silly. They wanted to ride bikes or play ball, but

I was different. I liked clowns. That summer, I watched every episode at noon, without fail.

Bozo found our reservation, pulled our room key from the pegboard behind the counter, and handed it over after having me sign in. My credit card was already on file from the online booking. There was no minibar in the room, but we could charge meals and gift shop items to our room—and even use it at the vending machine, which I noticed across the lobby, was blessedly stocked with cold beer.

Bozo motioned to Krusty the Clown (of The Simpsons fame) working the lobby to grab our bags and escort us to our room. I waved him off politely, offering a tip. "We've just got two small bags—we can take them," I said.

True to character, Krusty grumbled in mock protest, but I caught the grateful smile tugging beneath the greasepaint as the twenty slipped up his sleeve.

We dropped our bags off in the room—quick and simple—then, mercifully, Alison declared, "Let's eat first. We can explore the room, the hallways, and the shops after lunch."

No argument here.

Chapter 4

A Delicious Lunch

We thoroughly enjoyed the buffet in the dining room and even recognized a few familiar faces from past Halloween Misfits conventions. Most were either finishing up, already eating, or just grabbing a light lunch before heading off to explore, so Alison and I found a cozy table for two.

The room buzzed with laughter and merriment as clown servers worked their magic— telling jokes, performing tricks, and keeping the crowd entertained throughout the meal. One juggled pins while another appeared to flambé a whole pig— though it turned out to be an illusion. The actual dish was a mouthwatering Port Wine–Glazed Stuffed Roast Pork.

Some servers delivered dishes while riding wobbly tricycles, yet every cup and plate stayed perfectly in place thanks to magnetized trays. Not a drop spilled. The background music was lightly carnival-esque, just enough to set the mood without being irritating.

Lunch was served tableside, but the menu offered over a dozen rotating main courses and side dishes—all included in a single price. I was too hungry to be picky, so I sampled almost everything and was completely stuffed by the time we stood up, ready to explore the hotel.

As we exited the dining room, a sudden rush of icy air swept over us. Oddly, it didn't touch the concierge clown standing nearby—his bright hair unmoving, not even a wisp out of place. Alison and I exchanged a nervous laugh, brushing it off as one of the hotel's "haunted touches," though it left a strange feeling in the pit of my stomach.

Other guests left without any sign of the same cold draft, which only added to the weirdness. The concierge, clearly noting our unease, gestured toward several attractions.

"If you're lookin' to warm up, I'd recommend the replica museum or the gift shop where you'll find our miniatures," he said with an exaggerated wink.

We chose the gift shop and miniatures first—it had been the most talked-about feature in all the reviews we'd read.

"Danny, look here," Alison said excitedly, pointing to a colorful display. "It's a whole history of the Bozo the Clown show—including toys, books, even DVDs! You must find something to keep as a souvenir. I mean, this was the start of your clown career, too!"

She was completely absorbed, carefully lifting each item, turning it over, reading every word on the box like it was an ancient relic.

Unlike Alison—who could walk into a store and instantly zero in on the first thing that caught her eye, ignoring everything else until she was ready to move on to item (or category) number two—I was more methodical. Or maybe just overwhelmed.

I stood motionless, taking in the room crowded with glassy-eyed dolls, fading clown memorabilia, and unsettling replicas of history's most grotesque jesters. Despite my self-proclaimed status as a clown aficionado, something about the space felt deeply wrong. The walls seemed to waver at the edges—melting without dripping, like wax caught in a slow breath. Corners didn't quite meet where they should, angles felt just a hair off, and the entire room leaned subtly, as if the architecture itself couldn't decide what was up. Alison, somehow, didn't seem to notice.

Maybe it was the heavy lunch churning in my gut, or maybe the quiet frustration that rodeo clowns were once again left out of the narrative. Either way, a strange queasiness was tumbling through my body.

Leaning against the gift shop's packing desk for balance, I scanned the room again. Nowhere—

nowhere—was there a single rodeo clown of note. Not a photo, not a poster, not a figurine. For the first time since arriving, a knot of unease settled low in my stomach. Maybe we should've stayed at the Mizpah Hotel in town after all. It was notoriously haunted—featured on one of those History Channel Haunted Hotels episodes—but at least it didn't pretend to be something it wasn't.

Alison, meanwhile, was having the time of her life. She picked up every item that wasn't marked DO NOT TOUCH, completely absorbed, not noticing me or the weird energy in the room.

I wandered over to the French section, where displays of harlequins, Pierrot, and even a few mime clowns lined the shelves. About halfway down the aisle, a faint melody began to play. I had to strain to hear it at first—soft and eerie, like the tinkling of a music box from far away.

My first thought was that Alison had opened one, but before I could turn around, something brushed against my left shoulder.

I jerked and turned.

Pushed back against a shelf was a miniature theater stage, maybe two feet wide by two feet tall. Inside, a troupe of tiny clowns danced and performed tricks. I bent forward, squinting. There were no strings. No visible gears or motors. Their feet didn't move across anything mechanical that I could see— they just danced. Freely. Effortlessly.

As the music came to an abrupt stop, every clown on the stage turned its head in perfect unison—and stared straight at me.

I recoiled with a gasp, stumbling backward. My arm flailed behind me and collided with Alison, sending her crashing into a towering pile of clown dolls.

"Danny! What on earth has gotten into you?" she snapped, trying to right herself. "That bump made me knock everything off this huge display! You know if any of this was breakable, we'd be paying for it."

She stood and brushed herself off, her eyes darting to the You Break It, You Buy It sign hanging above the register. I helped her up with a sheepish tug and started re-stacking the fallen dolls, trying to slow the racing in my chest.

Alison, unfazed, said, "Anyway, just look what I found in the first aisle!"

She held up an old-school metal lunchbox. "It's the same one you said you had—the one with that famous picture of Bozo and Cookie the Clown on one side, and Bozo with the circus players and the Bozo's Circus drum on the other!"

Her eyes sparkled. "I think we should get this and use it to store all our favorite rodeo adventure photos."

I nodded, still dazed from the stages. Currently, those photos are taped over one another on our refrigerator in a cluttered mess. A real home for them—especially one wrapped in nostalgia—sounded just right.

She was admiring her find, commenting on everything she saw along with the price tags, but, looking back, all I could focus on was that area on the now-dark shelf. No stage. No dancing clowns. No music.

"Sure, Alison, whatever you think," I said, just to get her to move along the aisle. I lingered a bit, still wondering where the stage could have gone. I hadn't even noticed she'd left—or maybe just wandered into another section. Now, with the hairs on the back of my neck standing upright, I just wanted to get out of that aisle as fast as possible.

Alison pulled me over to the scary clown aisle and started chatting about all the movies she'd already seen, the books she'd already read, and how nothing new ever really represented clowns well. Then she started musing that maybe she should write a history of clowns—after all, she was a history teacher. I just nodded and followed along.

Eventually, she wore herself out on the shopping spree, and we headed for the front desk. She handed the desk clerk our room key and the lunchbox. "Would you be able to add that to our room charges? And send it on to our room?" she asked in an almost snobby tone.

But the Bozo receptionist just smiled and confirmed, "Absolutely, we can do that, Mrs. Harrison. I'll have it delivered right away."

Alison motioned toward my billfold and pointed at the $5 bills. Without blinking, I handed her as many as I had. She gave two to the clerk, saying, "I'm not sure if you ever get tips, but here, this is for you."

Then, in a strange show of confidence, she asked again, "Do you ever get tips?" She seemed to double down on her assumption, as if doubting they received any. "Well, anyway, here, this is for you for being so helpful."

"And would you please give the other bill to the delivery person?" she added. Almost embarrassed by the whole exchange, her face now a mix of confusion and guilt, she turned her attention to the replica room and mumbled, "Thank you."

The clerk looked at me with a bit of a twinkle in his eye and asked, "Are you okay, Mr. Harrison?" It was the subtle smirk that scared me into abruptly turning on my heel and hurrying after Alison at the Replica entry door.

Before I got too far, the desk clerk interrupted me.

"Sir, might I suggest you and Mrs. Harrison head over and check in at the event desk?"

He glanced at us with a knowing air.

"Afterward, you might want to take a walk around the hotel grounds to see the sights during daylight hours. It'll be dusk soon, and that's when the event activities begin. There'll be plenty of time tomorrow to see all the replicas of the themed rooms here at the hotel."

Alison, who had been listening from the entry door, thought this was a splendid idea. After stopping at the vending machine for two bottles of water, she led me out the front door and across the street.

"Danny, all the guidebooks say the best view of the hotel is from this side of the street. You get a wonderful view of the themed building," Alison said, pulling out her phone. She began snapping pictures from every angle, then switched to video mode.

"Go stand next to the clown at the door," she said. I moved as if on autopilot, still a bit unsettled from my experience in the gift shop.

When the video was done, Alison turned to me.

"Danny, what is the matter? You look like a lost little boy! Isn't this just the best motel—especially for you, a rodeo clown? Now smile so I can send a picture to my sister!"

I tried to smile, but even that felt crooked. I just couldn't get my balance back.

Alison pleaded with me to climb the tower steps so we could get a better view from the second and third floors. To me, they looked rickety and unsafe, but according to her guidebooks, there were a few "must-see" details to spot from each level for a complete Clown Motel experience. So up the stairs we went.

Though the weird feeling from the gift shop still lingered, I began to think I'd imagined it. I started to listen to Alison as she eagerly pointed things out. She was clearly having a great time. I was glad we had come—glad to see her happy.

After about thirty minutes, we descended the tower and walked down the street, though the stroll turned out to be a bit of a letdown. All we found was the graveyard we'd be touring privately later that evening. Across the street from the graveyard entrance was a row of business storefronts, their windows lined with old movie posters.

All featured clowns—some evil, some funny, some strangely tender—but all were a bit tattered. We studied the posters, but the storefronts themselves were dark, their interiors completely hidden.

We meandered back toward the hotel, noting that the parking lot was nearly full now.

It was October, and as we turned to look westward down the dusty road, the sunset exploded with extraordinary blues, oranges, yellows, and reds. The colors floated across the sky, interrupted only by a few distant rocky hills. A lonely, wavy road bisected the view, disappearing into the darkening horizon.

The hotel sign flickered on, its blinking lights cutting through the gray-blue dusk.

Back inside, we quickly caught up with our convention group, checked in at the event registration desk, and picked up our badges.

We were officially beginning our Halloween Misfits Weekend.

Chapter 5
Good Friends

Upon entering the main bar, we recognized a few of the same folks we'd seen at lunch—then heard our names called out. Turning around, we spotted Alex and Mindy, friends from past Halloween events. Alex, like me, is a rodeo clown, though he competes on a different prize circuit. Mindy works as a hair stylist, which allows her the same scheduling flexibility as Alison. Fortunately, Mindy and Alison get along really well—they have a lot in common.

Alex was the only other rodeo clown we knew of attending this event, though we hoped a few more might show up before the weekend was over.

"When did you arrive?" Mindy asked, giving Alison a hug as they started scanning the room for four open seats. The two of them chatted away while Alex and I made our way over to the bartender.

"Two beers, please," I said, placing my room key on the counter.

"You okay, Danny?" Alex asked, giving me a once-over. "You look like you've seen a ghost—or maybe ate something you shouldn't have."

"Yeah," I said, pausing as I glanced back toward the lobby. "I'm okay. Just a long day driving in from Vegas. We came in yesterday, stayed overnight, caught a show, and got to bed late. Probably drank too much and definitely ate too much before the show. But it was a great night. I felt fine this morning, and now—here we are."

"Sir, your beers," said the bartender—a tall, spindly guy who looked like he might be in college, though maybe not. He glanced toward the tip jar as he handed us our drinks.

I dropped in a twenty-dollar bill, hoping he'd remember Alex and me and give us good service for the rest of the weekend.

Alex raised his bottle toward the jar with a nod. "We got in this afternoon—about an hour ago. Of course, we had to head straight into the gift shop. I think Mindy might've bought out the place."

"Yeah, we went in too," I said, hesitating. I wasn't sure if I should mention what I saw, especially since Alex didn't seem to have had the same experience.

Then Alex asked, "Danny, did you get a weird feeling when you came into the hotel?"

I answered cautiously, "Not when we first came in… but when I went into the gift shop, yeah, I did."

"Did you see anything weird?"

I knew I must've sounded ridiculous. But if there was anyone I could tell, it was Alex. He's the sanest guy I know. We'd learned the rodeo clown profession together—faced down bulls, jumped broncos, and herded sheep away from kids in our early days.

What I saw had to be my imagination… unless Alex saw it too.

We set our beers on a nearby round stand-up table, just far enough from the bar to avoid nosy ears. Neither of us took a sip. Alex stared silently at his bottle for several minutes. Finally, he picked it up and said, "Let's go find the girls." I was pretty sure something had happened to him, but he wasn't ready to talk about it yet. I could wait.

Chapter 6
Graveyard

At another tabletop, Mindy and Alison were busy comparing the upcoming November and December travel itineraries for Alex and me, scanning calendars to see if their paths might cross at any of the same rodeo shows before Christmas. Neither Alex nor I said a word; we simply observed the room in quiet curiosity.

Eventually, the event coordinator, Nick Stanton, stood and began outlining the weekend's agenda. After dinner, we'd be treated to a private tour of the cemetery. The following day promised a surprise—an adults-only fun house and carnival set to open at noon, followed by dinner and dancing late into the night. The festivities would conclude with a breakfast buffet on Sunday morning for those still in town. Nick covered a few practical housekeeping notes and then invited us all to proceed to the dining room for the evening meal. There had been no specific mention of activities for clowns—yet glancing around, it became evident that nearly everyone in the room was some variety of clown.

Once we were all seated—eight tables, four guests to a table—Nick rose again, thanked everyone for making the journey, and pressed a button with a dramatic flourish, declaring, "Let the festivities begin!" This weekend was ours, for once—a chance for the clowns to revel instead of orchestrate the revelry for others.

Instantly, the candles on each table ignited in unison. The overhead lights dimmed several notches, cloaking the room in an eerie, celebratory glow. Then came the servers, one per table, not clad in clown attire but transformed into terrifying creatures that looked as though they had stepped off a major Hollywood horror set. At the corner of the room, a curtain pulled back to reveal a live band decked out in full Kiss regalia. Their music swelled—just loud enough to set a playful, Halloween-infused atmosphere—as we turned our attention to the set menu. Each table setting featured a placard detailing the multi-course meal we were about to enjoy.

Welcome to the World-Famous Clown Motel

Tonopah, Nevada

HALLOWEEN MISFITS WEEKEND

MENU – Friday Evening

First Course

Eyeball Soup – a delicious beef broth- based soup with enchanting spices, eyeballs (meatballs), and bones (al dente pasta)

Second Course

Red Whining Salad – house salad served with fragrant herb infused house vinaigrette, topped with crunchy tidbits.

Third Course

Wine infused Spaniard chicken, with a sliced beet, rutabaga, and turnip medley, alongside potatoes au gratin.

Dessert

A plethora of devilishly bewitching petit fours accompanied by an open bar – open until morning's light.

Bon Appetit

The waiters emerged with wine—red, naturally, in perfect harmony with the menu—and as glasses were poured, the quiet murmur of conversation at each table gradually grew into a lively, indistinguishable din punctuated by laughter.

After leaving two open bottles of wine at each table, the servers returned from the kitchen bearing the first course: Eyeball Soup. The girls dove in without hesitation, giggling over the cleverness of the edible irises and veined meatballs floating among perfectly cooked al dente noodles.

But Alex and I were seeing something different. The "eyes"—painstakingly crafted to resemble the real thing—seemed to stare back at us. No matter how we rotated our bowls, the gaze of the eyes followed. Alex bent down to smell it, only to recoil and wrinkle his nose before pushing the bowl away with slow, deliberate disgust. Then, with only the slightest turn of his neck, he met my eye. Behind his practiced calm, a flash of horror broke through.

I looked down again. Despite myself, my hand reached for the spoon. I felt drawn to it—irresistibly. But before I could take a bite, Alex clasped my wrist and squeezed firmly until the spoon clattered from my fingers. Just like that, the pull dissipated. I pushed my bowl away too, reached for my beer, and took a long swallow, grounding myself with the malty bitter taste.

Moments later, the servers returned—now two per table. As one cleared the soup bowls and utensils, the other presented the next course: salad. They laughed and joked as they worked, placing silver gravy boats between us, each filled with a deep crimson wine vinaigrette that shimmered with an almost too-perfect sheen.

The salad itself was unremarkable—mixed greens and vegetables—but instead of croutons, it was topped with strange fried shreds. They resembled clam strips or stir-fried noodles but didn't look particularly appetizing.

The girls, still chatting and laughing, immediately dug in.

Just as I reached for the dressing, Alex once again intervened, his hand halting mine mid-motion. His eyes weren't on me—they were scanning the room. I followed his gaze. Guests were pouring dressing over their salads so liberally it pooled in their bowls like broth. Across from us, the girls had emptied both vinaigrette boats, their salads soaked and glistening as they slurped them up with shocking enthusiasm—like they hadn't eaten in days.

When I looked down at my own plate, I noticed something else: the fried strips weren't just greasy—they were twitching. Subtly, faintly—but unmistakably. And beneath the pungent tang of vinegar, there was a hidden odor—faint, but hauntingly familiar. It was the smell of blood and sweat—of the arena—of the men we'd seen gored by bulls. Alex and I knew it well; we'd helped corral the chaos, driving panicked livestock into pens while medics rushed to fallen riders. It was the scent of trauma.

The hunger clawing at my stomach was undeniable, but I shoved the salad away. Alex's face had turned grim—his expression was no longer just concerned. It was fear.

What was this meal?

Around us, the room had erupted in celebration—guests chattering, laughing, devouring every bite with ravenous delight. No, not just eating. Consuming. Gorging. There was something almost grotesque about it, a feverish gluttony that bordered on the unhinged.

The servers returned—now three assigned to each table. One cleared the salad plates and utensils; the second placed the main course in front of each diner; and the third, dressed in the most grotesque mask and costume imaginable, was the bartender. Each ensemble looked crafted to haunt dreams—a twisted blend of carnival and nightmare.

The bartenders leaned in with exaggerated flair and asked if anyone would like to try the signature cocktail of the evening: The Clown Hair Grimace, a concoction designed specifically for this year's party. Without hesitation, the girls exclaimed a unified and enthusiastic yes, not even bothering to ask what was in it. Alex and I declined politely, requesting bottled beers—still capped. This dinner was growing stranger by the minute.

Before us sat the main course, at first glance, it appeared to be a simple roasted chicken—predictable, given that clowns and rubber chicken jokes were practically synonymous. But beside it lay a peculiar arrangement of thinly sliced rounds. Some were stark white, etched or dyed with red bullseye spirals. Others were deep red with white spirals, like a grotesque inversion. Perhaps beets and turnips as described on the menu? But the ghostly pallor of the turnips and the translucent, sickly hue of the rutabagas—somewhere between spoiled cream and bruised peach—were unsettling. They were fanned out with surgical precision, dull in color yet hypnotic in their grotesqueness. I looked away.

The potatoes seemed safe—standard au gratin, bubbling in a small oval ramekin with all the familiar fixings: sour cream, butter, bacon bits, and chives. At this point, I was starving. While Mindy and Alison were served their rainbow-hued Clown Hair Grimace, Alex and I received our beers—mercifully sealed and accompanied by frosted glasses.

Servers now hovered between each pair of guests, attending them like personal buffet valets. Platters continued to circulate, and the air grew thick with the cloying scent of roasted meat, rich sauces, and something else—something metallic and primal.

I could no longer resist. I grabbed my spoon and dug into the potatoes, lifting a heaping bite to my mouth. But just before it touched my lips, Alex tipped his beer, sending it cascading across my plate and startling me out of my trance. The spoon clattered against the ceramic, my appetite vanishing in an instant.

Only then did I realize the room had gone nearly silent. The only sounds were the clinking of utensils and a chorus of chewing—wet, exaggerated, animalistic chewing. No conversation. No laughter. Just gluttony. Diners hunched over their plates, shoveling food with frenzied abandon. Plates were being refilled before they were empty. Guests stared at their servers like predators eyeing prey.

And then, I saw him—Nick Stanton. He was the only person not eating. The only one looking at us. And the only one who had clearly heard the sound of the beer bottle tipping.

Alex stood, nudging his chair back and gently grabbing my arm. With casual ease, he said to the girls, "Can we get you anything from the bar? Dan and I are going for another beer."

They didn't respond. Didn't even look up. It was as if he hadn't spoken at all. Their eyes were glazed over, their movements mechanical, their expressions locked in some euphoric stupor.

Something was very wrong.

We slipped out through the labyrinth of servers and bartenders moving in synchronized chaos, navigating around the tables like a macabre ballet. As we exited, a cool gust of air greeted us— almost as if the building itself was pushing us out, guiding us away from the madness and into solitude.

Now in the lobby, we sat in silence on a faded velvet couch, far from the front desk and the costumed baggage clowns milling about. We cracked open two beers each from a vending machine and drank without a word, trying to process what we'd just witnessed.

Neither of us dared speak the thought clawing at the back of our minds. Not what was being served… but who. But to even say it out loud would be to give it power—to accept it as possible. And surely, that thought was insane. It had to be.

From the distance, we heard Nick's voice over the loudspeaker, making another announcement. Soon after, the dining room doors opened, and the crowd spilled into the lobby. Their faces were flushed, their movements languid but content.

"I swear, that was the best meal I've ever had," one man said.

Another chimed in, "I cannot wait for dessert. After the cemetery tour, they're serving it in the lounge."

Alex and I looked at each other.

We were not staying for dessert.

Soon, Nick appeared at the front entrance, standing alongside the hotel owner—who now looked more like a spectral tour guide in his long black coat—while Alex stood silently beside them.

"We'll begin our cemetery tour now," Nick announced. "It's filled with many people—not world-famous, perhaps—but each with a story, each touched by something… unusual during their time here in Tonopah. The cemetery is quite old, so please be cautious. There are uneven paths, exposed roots, and crumbling headstones."

The hotel owner nodded solemnly before Nick continued, "As you enter, you'll find a flashlight waiting for you. Please aim it at the ground while walking—we want to avoid any twisted ankles. We'll pause together at each grave of interest to hear what our guide has to share."

Nick scanned the crowd, counting heads with a practiced eye. "Alright then, let's move out—and don't forget, dessert will be waiting for us back in the lounge afterward!"

With that, Nick and the hotelier-turned-guide pivoted and stepped through the doors, heading toward the cemetery just beyond the hotel grounds.

One by one, the guests followed—still dressed in their clownish costumes, but moving with such quiet obedience that they seemed more like sheep than revelers.

Alex and I lingered a moment, scanning for the girls. We spotted them near the back of the group, laughing and giggling with an edge of strangeness to their smiles, their eyes glassy and unreadable.

"Did you two find something better to eat?" Mindy asked with an airy tone, cocking her head as if she already knew the answer.

I didn't reply. Instead, I nodded toward the moving procession and said, "We'd better catch up, or we'll miss the tour."

Without another word, Mindy and Alison turned, linking arms and drifting forward—cheerfully marching into the night as if summoned by something unseen.

Alex and I exchanged a glance. Whatever this was, it wasn't just dinner, and it wasn't just a tour.

It was something else entirely.

Chapter 7
The Tour

The entrance to the cemetery was surprisingly well-maintained. A polished plaque detailed a brief history of Tonopah and the various groups of people buried there. As we approached, Nick did another headcount, nodding with approval once satisfied that all were present. He turned things over to the hotel owner, who stepped forward in his long coat and began the tour in a practiced tone.

He explained that the cemetery held the remains of miners and local townsfolk—store owners, saloonkeepers, ladies of the evening, and others who had come to seek their fortunes during the silver boom. More recently deceased residents, he added, were buried in the newer town cemetery just beside the historic Mizpah Hotel. The original Mizpah, he told us, had been constructed at the height of the boom but fell into decline as quickly as the town itself, over the course of about fifteen years. From barren desert to booming town to modest outpost—Tonopah had seen it all.

The Clown Motel, he went on, was relatively recent—built in 1985 to house the extensive clown memorabilia collection of Clarence David. Since then, it had changed hands multiple times but remained a roadside curiosity and had been featured in countless articles about haunted hotels, ghost towns, and offbeat Americana.

Alex and I were the last to take our flashlights and trail the group. Along the way, we pointed out to each other the elaborate Halloween decorations scattered throughout the graveyard—life-sized figures, enormous spiders, carved pumpkins, and eerie lanterns. Oddly, neither of us had seen a single decoration earlier that day. The lighting was sparse, and our flashlights were constantly scanning for potholes, gnarled roots, or uneven gravestones. It kept our eyes down more often than up.

At the first stop, the owner launched into the story of James "Old JJ" Butler and his wife Bertha. They had been the first to discover silver in the region. Bertha, clearly the sharper of the two, filed eight claims in their name and brokered deals with other prospectors, eventually securing a 25% share of the profits from all finds within their claim zones. By 1921, the Butlers had sold their claims, the mines having yielded over $150 million in silver, copper, gold, and lead before shutting down near the end of World War II. Though the mining boom had collapsed, Tonopah lingered on as a pit stop between Las Vegas and Reno as casinos took on the role of triumphant herald to those looking for new gold in gambling.

The guide shared more as we moved through the cemetery, describing how injuries were rampant among miners and how their families often struggled to survive. It was the saloon ladies, he said with a touch of reverence, who stepped in to help. There was a quiet symbiosis between the men, their families, and these "ladies of the night," who became cornerstones of the town's strange but functioning society.

As the group drifted toward the next cluster of graves, Alex and I lagged behind, taking time to investigate some of the graveyard's decorations more closely. We walked in short bursts—five or six steps—then paused to sweep our flashlights across the grounds. That's when we noticed: the "decorations" weren't props. These were bodies—adults in costume, yes, but dressed in horrifyingly convincing states of decay. One had crudely severed limbs. Another had no head. A third twitched with stiff, unnatural movements, its motions erratic and jerking.

We took a cautious step closer to the nearest figure—its body slick with blood, bent awkwardly at the base of a tombstone. Before we could get too close, Nick's voice cut through the dark: "Hey there, you two—try to stay with the group. We don't want anyone getting left behind or breaking an ankle!"

We looked at each other, then at the body still slowly writhing near the stone. Reluctantly, we backed away and rejoined the group, which had just reached the next stop. Nick moved ahead to resume guiding the others, and we found ourselves momentarily left alone again.

Nearby, a corpse-like figure was slumped over a tombstone. Drawn forward, we crept closer. Even in the dark, the details were disturbingly vivid. A leg, severed just below the pelvis, still seemed to ooze blood. The eyes—if they had been eyes—were now sunken pits, lids closed over hollow sockets. It was the most realistic makeup I'd ever seen—too realistic.

Just as we were leaning in, the group suddenly turned and began doubling back—heading toward a large, moonlit mausoleum behind us. We were caught in the shuffle and pushed to the side, now no longer trailing the group but off to its flank. The crowd's oohs and aahs, as boisterous as at a fireworks show, hinted they were seeing things neither Alex nor I had seen.

We aimed our flashlights toward the far end of the clearing. Strangely, the bodies that had been scattered along the edges of the cemetery were now gone—or at least, no longer within our line of sight.

We couldn't speak freely, not with the guests still under whatever spell held them so rapt. Alex leaned close to my ear and whispered, "Nick thinks we're in the middle now—he won't be keeping tabs. Let's wait for everyone to pass, then hang back. I want to check out that mausoleum. I swear the door's cracked open."

I turned my light toward the shadowed entrance. Sure enough, the heavy stone door was slightly ajar, just enough to see the edge of its inner frame, unlatched and welcoming.

Five minutes later, Alex leaned in again, voice barely audible. "I'll go check the door. You cover me. If Nick starts heading back this way, bend over and pretend to take off your shoe—say you've got a rock in it. He'll be focused on you and won't see me by the wall. If he asks, say you think I'm already up ahead with the others. Got it?"

I nodded, heart pounding. Whatever was inside that mausoleum, Alex intended to find out.

And I wasn't about to let him do it alone.

I nodded an ok and began to look for Nick in the crowd. My plan was to make sure he saw me walking with the group before I stopped and bent down. This way, he'd assume I was with the group, giving Alex a few extra seconds to look inside the building.

Chapter 8
The Kitchen

The group erupted in laughter at the guide's last joke before he waved everyone toward the next set of graves. I glanced up just in time to meet Nick's eyes. I made sure to laugh—an easy, hollow thing—bumping along with the crowd, giving every impression I was just another clown enjoying the show. Nick gave a small nod, turned away, and resumed his role at the head of the group.

Perfect.

Alex slipped toward the side of the mausoleum, vanishing into the shadowed edge. I stayed behind, keeping an eye on Nick. Just as he scanned the stragglers, I pointed toward my shoe, tucked my flashlight under my chin, and bent down like I was tying my laces. Satisfied I was accounted for, he turned his focus elsewhere.

We were free.

Alex crept to the heavy stone door and eased it open just enough to shine his flashlight inside. He sucked in a sharp breath.

I darted over and peered past him.

Inside—what should've been a dust-laden crypt—stood something far worse. A clown, fully dressed, complete with wig, greasepaint, and costume, lay half-hewn on a stone slab. Blood trickled in rhythmic pulses from the torso, funneling down into a rusted pot below. The severed left arm and leg were tossed carelessly at the foot of the platform. There was no movement—none that I could detect—and no sounds apart from the soft, wet drip of blood.

Alex stumbled back in horror.

I staggered out with him, both of us too stunned to speak.

That's when Alex caught his foot on a twisted root just outside the door. His flashlight flew from his hand, bounced off a nearby tombstone, and began flickering violently. I lunged forward, managing to slow his fall, but not before my own flashlight skittered out of my grip—straight through the crack in the mausoleum door, where it landed just inside the crypt.

The noise wasn't deafening, but in the heavy silence of the graveyard, it may as well have been gunfire.

Nick appeared a moment later, rounding the corner. His face was impassive as he took in the scene—Alex on his back, our flashlights in disarray, the crypt door slightly ajar and glowing with a strange, flickering light.

He sighed.

Stepping closer, he looked down at us and, with eerie calm, asked, "Did you two have dinner?"

I glanced at Alex, confused. What the hell kind of question was that?

Neither of us answered.

Nick nodded, sighed again, and pulled out his phone. He tapped out a short message—too short—and put it away.

"You two should grab your flashlights and close the mausoleum door," he said.

But instead of helping, Nick nudged me forward—hard—just enough to push me back into the open doorway. At the same time, he reached for Alex's arm as if to help him up. But instead of pulling, he simply shifted aside. Alex stumbled, crashing into me, and the both of us fell back into the crypt.

"What the hell, Nick?" I barked, reaching out to steady myself—and Alex.

And then, with an awful grinding sound of ancient stone, the door shut.

We were in darkness.

One flashlight remained—mine—still casting a faint glow from where it lay inside the crypt. The clown's body lay motionless nearby, its blood still seeping into the waiting pot. The silence was heavy, almost pressing. Our voices echoed faintly as we pounded on the stone from the inside.

"Nick!" I shouted. "Open the damn door!"

Alex joined in: "This isn't funny! Let us out!"

Nothing. Not even footsteps outside. Only the dull, muffled thump of our fists against the thick stone.

I turned to the body again, drawn back to its grotesque realism. This… this was no Halloween prop.

"Alex," I said, voice trembling, "this… this is real."

He was already moving, searching the walls with the dim light. "There has to be another way out," he muttered. "A vent, a crack, something—"

There wasn't.

Panic started to rise in my throat.

Alex turned back to me, the horror finally registering on his face. "Dan," he said slowly, "did you hear what Nick asked us?"

I didn't answer.

"He asked if we ate dinner," Alex pressed, eyes wide. "Why? Why would he ask that now?"

I just stared, stunned, mind blank.

"Dan!" he barked, grabbing my shoulders and shaking me. When I didn't respond, he slapped me across the face—hard. "Snap out of it!"

"I think…" I swallowed. "I think he means to leave us here. As punishment. To scare us. Because we skipped the meal."

Alex shook his head, eyes dark. "No. That's not it. He wasn't mad."

I blinked.

"He was checking," Alex said. "He wanted to know if we were already fed. If we were full."

We both turned slowly toward the clown on the slab.

That was no wax dummy. No artfully mangled mannequin.

That had been a person. And now it was food.

Before I could collapse entirely, a deep creaking sound echoed inside the crypt, not from the door—but from below the slab. The stone lid of the platform began to move, cracking open from within. A thin beam of light stretched across the walls, growing wider with every passing second.

Alex yanked me into the furthest corner and switched off the flashlight. We held our breath.

The slab finished shifting. From inside the chamber, something emerged.

A server.

One of our servers—from dinner.

He rose from within the tomb, holding a bright, focused flashlight that swept slowly around the chamber walls until it landed on us.

His mouth curled into an inhuman grin.

Two more heads followed, rising from the stone—both servers as well. All three were massive, impossibly so, and now stood hunched beneath the crypt ceiling.

Their painted faces had changed. The cheer was gone. What remained was hunger, devotion, and purpose.

They advanced.

BOOK TWO
ALISON

Chapter 1
Breakfast

Mindy was with me at breakfast when Nick came over to check on us, as he'd been doing at all the other tables.

"Good morning, ladies! I hope you enjoyed the cemetery tour last night. I didn't see either of you at the dessert bar afterward," Nick remarked with his usual cheer.

"Oh yes, you wouldn't have known," I replied, pausing, the muted concern I'd carried all morning flickering faintly through my mind— though I wasn't sure it registered on my face. Nick didn't seem to notice, but that thought passed quickly.

"Alex and Danny left notes for us at the front desk last night," I continued. "They said they were heading into town..." My brain faltered, caught briefly on that detail.

Then, with a conscious nudge, I added, "…to go to the Mizpah and meet a few friends from previous years. They told us not to wait up."

Drawing a much-needed breath and letting the scent of the rich breakfast settle me, I finished—perhaps more drained than I realized—"After that, I was just too tired for dessert. Did you go down, Mindy?"

And with that, I exhaled a low but pronounced sigh and turned my attention to the steak and eggs in front of me.

"No," Mindy replied frankly. "My feet were killing me, and after the long walk and that scrumptious meal, I was completely wiped out." She punctuated the thought with a hearty bite of the meat beside her eggs.

"I'm surprised Danny didn't make it back last night," I said with a shrug. "But if I had to guess, I'd say he and Alex found a few old rodeo friends who couldn't get rooms here, had one too many shots, and he's probably passed out on a couch somewhere."

I was surprised by my own calm, nonchalant tone—but somehow, it felt entirely appropriate.

"Well then, I guess we won't need to keep breakfast open for them," Nick said, glancing toward the head waiter before turning back to us. "If they show up later and still want to eat, they can ask the front desk for a breakfast platter even if the buffet's closed," he added, looking from Mindy to me. "You'll let them know?"

Mindy spoke up, "Rodeo clown life is a rough one—they drink hard after a competition ends. I agree with Alison. They probably tied one on, or we'd have already gotten a call from the local hospital."

I knew Mindy well enough to sense her silent gratitude—to the stars, to luck, or to the Lord—that Alex and Danny had made it through another rodeo unscathed.

"And it's not so unusual for Alex to crash somewhere after a long day at the rodeo," she added with a shrug before diving into her next bite. "I'm not worried."

"It's not typical for Danny," I admitted, "but I wouldn't be surprised if they show up before noon looking for lunch, a shower, and a change of clothes."

We both chuckled and changed the subject to the delightfully creamy eggs. Too content and too engaged with our plates to chat much more, we sat listening to the happy clamor around the dining room—

"The buffet was especially delicious this morning."

"The Bloody Marys were superb!"

"What's in this food? It's fabulous!"

"Excuse me—I have to go back for seconds!"

"Can I get the recipes?"

Nick grinned, dipped his head to us both, and moved on to the next table, while Mindy and I returned to the buffet for another round.

After a few more stops, I spotted Nick again at the front of the room, where he began his morning announcements.

"Good morning, everyone. I trust you all had a great time last night, enjoyed the tour and dessert?" Nick said, barely finishing before the room all clapped and hollered their hoorays.

"Great to hear it," he said. "On to today. First, there's a haunted house!"

The room erupted again into applause, cheers, and bursts of laughter between bites.

"It'll be open from noon until 7 p.m.," he continued. "Do you plan to go through the house several times as the rooms change constantly throughout the day?"

Nick laughed along with the crowd, raising his arms to settle the noise. "There will also be all the regular carnival rides, food stalls, and games," he added, pausing briefly. "With prizes!"

Another round of cheers and hoots rose like a tide.

When the crowd quieted, Nick went on, "Dinner tonight will be an outdoor barbecue with all the fixings, running until about nine. Music and dancing begin at eight and will last until the last guest drops… which might be tomorrow, if you're up for it."

He paused again while the forty or so convention-goers chatted excitedly among themselves, then shared a few final notes.

"We've got two bands lined up. They'll take turns every hour," he said. "And raffles will be held throughout the evening to raise funds for next year's bash. Bring your room keys—yes, your keys!—

we've arranged for those to work as a simple payment method."

With a final grin and a theatrical wave, Nick exited the dining room, leaving everyone to enjoy the rest of their breakfast.

Sated and in high spirits, Mindy and I mingled with the other guests, all of us ambling toward the lobby with full bellies and easy laughter.

It was only eleven, so we decided to make a second visit to the gift shop. Much was the same, though today a few new curiosities had appeared. Most intriguing was a stage featuring clown puppets.

A life-sized version of one of the many smaller puppets stood near a sign that read the miniatures would be available for purchase soon.

The clowns were mesmerizing—ornately costumed, their makeup lavish and theatrical, covering them completely. Only their eyes remained human, just barely. Even their mouths were obscured with thick paste and makeup.

As we approached the stage, the puppets began to move. No strings, no rods—just smooth, unnerving motion, their feet scarcely brushing the floor.

Two of them danced with a wistful joy, dressed and made up as sad clowns yet spinning with gaiety to the tune of haunting carnival music, reminiscent of the previous evening.

We watched for a time, caught between fascination and mild unease, then moved on. As we stepped away, the puppets slowly lost their momentum and crumpled against each other in a quiet heap. Sad faces matching their wilted physiques.

After browsing the rest of the shop, we passed the stage once more. This time, the clowns had changed—new costumes, new movements, but just as lively and uncanny.

We lingered briefly, then continued on. It was nearly noon, and a fleeting sense of unease rippled through me—but just as quickly, it passed.

Chapter 2

Alone

"Mindy, I'm going up to my room to get Danny. After a proper scolding for giving me a fright, he'll probably collapse into a nap—if he's not already out cold. If you'd like, we can meet in the lobby around one."

"Sounds good! But I'll be there—with or without a husband!" Mindy called over her shoulder with a mischievous cackle, already strolling down the hallway.

I opened the door, fully expecting to hear either the low rumble of snoring or the hum of the shower—either would have soothed the gnawing agitation that had been building since our second pass through the gift shop. That uneasy sense, like a shadow darting across the sun, swept over me again—then vanished, soundlessly, as before.

Something was off here. Just as something had been off there, at the puppet stage, I couldn't quite pinpoint what had made the hairs on my arms rise, but they had. Maybe it was the miniature puppet stages that had appeared out of nowhere—each unique and unsettling—or maybe it was the fact that Mindy and I had been right in the next aisle and hadn't seen anyone come in and set them up.

Whatever it was, that, and now this, didn't sit right.

The room looked undisturbed—eerily so. The bed was neatly made, and a note rested atop it:

Thank you, Alison.

Not The Harrisons.

Not Alison and Danny.

Not even Mr. and Mrs. Harrison.

Just Alison.

The note went on:

Have a wonderful afternoon and evening.

And beneath it, a single chocolate truffle wrapped in gold foil, labeled:

Compliments of the Clown Motel.

Only one truffle. Not two.

Had Danny already come and gone?

I searched the room again, slower this time. Nothing was out of place—except for the absence of Danny. I checked the closet. Everything seemed normal. Still, my stare lingering on one of his shirts, almost certain it was the one he'd worn last night. But Danny's clothes tended to look alike, so I couldn't say for sure.

Uneasy, I called the front desk.

"Any messages for me?" I asked.

"No, ma'am," the clerk replied cheerfully. "But the carnival's just getting started—you won't want to miss it!"

I cut him off. "Do you have the phone number for the Mizpah Hotel?"

"Yes, of course," he answered. I scribbled it down quickly but then said, frustrated, "Actually, could you just connect me, please?"

"Certainly, Alison. One moment."

The silence that followed stretched into what felt like an eternity before a voice finally came through:

"Thank you for calling the Mizpah Hotel. How may I help you?"

"Good morning. This is Alison Harrison, calling from the Clown Motel. I was wondering—do any of your guests happen to be attending the Halloween Misfits event here?"

There was a pause. "No, I don't believe any of our guests are attending an event at the Clown Motel."

That was odd. I pressed on. "Did you happen to see someone who fits my husband's description? He's five-foot-ten, brown hair brown eyes. He may have arrived last night with another man, Alex Sawyer. Similar build, but sandy blond hair and blue eyes. Probably came around ten."

"No," the clerk replied. "No one matching those descriptions came in last night, and I was at the front desk from noon until ten."

"Could you have missed them? Maybe they arrived after your shift?"

"I don't think so, ma'am. After 10 p.m., anyone arriving without a key uses the wall phone by the entrance. That rings my personal cell. I would've come down to verify their identity and either let them in, register them, or connect them with the guest they were visiting. It's our policy, especially for after-hours hotel access. If they went into the bar, they would have gone through the public entrance, and I would not have seen them."

Now I was no longer simply worried—I was furious. "Alright, thank you," I said curtly and hung up.

I immediately dialed Mindy. "Have you heard from Alex? I've got nothing from Danny, and I just called the Mizpah—they haven't seen anyone matching either Danny or Alex's description."

Mindy hesitated. "No, but… it wouldn't be unusual for Alex to have, well… found himself a lady for the evening and disappeared for a day or two. Or even a week. I know that sounds awful, and maybe you didn't suspect, but that's how our marriage works these days. He goes his way, I go mine—sometimes, we go together."

She continued quickly, "He left the car keys here, and since we only brought one bag, if he's not back by tomorrow morning, I'll just pack up and head back to Winnemucca."

My mind spun. "Mindy, that's nuts. Alex wouldn't do that! And Dan—he better not have done that! I mean, how could he just leave me here like this?"

Mindy's voice came through, calm but firm, trying to anchor me. "Alison, I'll be right over. You're spiraling, and we don't know anything yet. Hold tight, okay?"

But I wasn't hearing her. I wasn't listening. I was pacing, the phone, a dead, intermittent dial tone in my hand.

Could Danny have done the same thing? He was gone a lot for work—sometimes didn't call—but he always texted. Or came home the next day. Maybe he just didn't want to spend the day with the "non-rodeo clowns." He hadn't been wild about this weekend in the first place—it was my idea, not his.

By the time Mindy knocked, I'd already torn through the room looking for the car keys and was now peering out the window, trying to spot our vehicle.

"Mindy," I blurted, throwing open the door, "I can't find the car keys, and I don't see our car—Danny must've taken it to the Mizpah. Can you grab yours? I need to get over there, just to see if the car's there. I need to know he's okay."

"I'm sure we can make it back before the carnival really gets going," I added, already in my coat. "Maybe we'll even pass them on the way."

Mindy gave me a steady look. "Alright, Alison. I'll get my keys. Meet you in the lobby."

Grabbing my purse, I went to leave a note at the front desk—only to see Nick standing nearby.

I marched right up to him. "Nick, what is going on at the Mizpah?" I demanded. "I called—they said there are no events, no guests coming here for the Halloween party, nothing! Where are all the other people that usually come to these Misfits weekends?"

Nick looked to Mindy as she arrived, a question in his eyes.

Mindy answered, "Nick, you know Alex and Danny left us notes saying they were heading to the Mizpah and not to wait up. They haven't come back, and we were just heading out to look for them. Alison's pretty upset, as you can see."

"You're damn right I'm upset!" I snapped. "And Nick here doesn't seem to know anything!"

Nick lifted a hand. "Actually, I just got back from the Mizpah. And I can assure you—there are convention-goers in town for the carnival."

He waved toward two men standing nearby. "Alison, meet Ralph and Emmanual—from Tampa. They're with the new Ringling Bros. relaunch."

"Hello, Ms. Alison," they said in unison, faint Spanish accents softening their syllables. They were identical. Same smile. Same eyes. Same hair. A mirrored pair.

"We had planned to work with Ringling before it closed in 2017," Ralph said.

Emmanual jumped in without pause, "But now it reopens—so we work."

Nick turned back to us. "Why don't you ladies get some lunch while I head over to the Mizpah myself? If I don't find Danny's car—the white Bronco with Arizona plates, right?" He looked to me.

I nodded, mouth dry.

"I'll check every bar, restaurant, and hotel in town," Nick promised. "And if they're still not there, I'll go straight to the police station. I'll call you as soon as I know anything. Meanwhile, if they come back here, you call me right away."

Nick gave us both a moment. "Sound good?"

Mindy nodded. "Yes. I think that makes the most sense. If they show up, we'll be here. If not, you'll find them."

I wasn't convinced. But I was starving. And the scent of grilled food, full as I was from the breakfast buffet, wafting in from the hallway, made my stomach groan.

"Thanks, Nick," I muttered. "We'll stay here. We'll sit near the lobby so I can rip into Danny the second he walks in—and Mindy can call you and let you know he's safe. That's fair." I turned toward the smell, suddenly lightheaded. "Come on, Mindy."

My head buzzed like static. As we walked, I faintly heard Nick call after us: "When they come back, you'll all want to start joining in the fun."

The buzzing persisted—but the hunger was stronger.

Chapter 3

No Nick

I kept casting glances toward the dining room door throughout lunch, even as I devoured the soup, salad, main course, and dessert over the course of the next hour. Oddly, I was ravenous—despite having eaten breakfast just a few hours earlier. But the food was simply too good to resist. From the soup course onward, neither of us had mentioned Alex or Danny, and Mindy actually seemed surprised when I finally brought them up. It appeared that no news was good news—a far cry from the concerns I'd voiced to Nick.

With my final bite of what the menu called Tapioca Pudding with Deep-Fried Cinnamon Sliver Surprises, I leaned back and requested one last glass of wine.

"For strength at the carnival," I quipped to Mindy, who burst out laughing.

The server returned, poured us each a fresh glass with dramatic flair, and after producing a seemingly endless stream of kerchiefs, presented us with two tickets to the carnival. With a rather unsettling clownish grin, the server asked, "Will there be anything else before you've concluded your lunch?"

We both replied, "No, thank you," each murmuring that, once again, this had likely been the best lunch we'd ever had. We plucked the tickets from the server's hand and rose to leave.

As we stepped through the dining room doors, I must've had a strange expression on my face, because Mindy tilted her head and asked, "Is something wrong, Alison? Did you forget something at the table?"

"No, no," I said, "Nothing comes to mind... but something does feel a little off."

Mindy chuckled. "Maybe it was that final glass of wine for the road!"

We both laughed and detoured to the ladies' room before making our way to the carnival. I thought I saw Nick—and though an odd shiver ran through me, I brushed it off, blaming the sensation on that last glass of red.

Chapter 4
Party Time

"Mindy! MINDY!" I cried out, nearly shrieking with delight. "Look! I've won! I've WON! And can you believe it—it's a Roomba! I've wanted one for so long! And look, this lovely clown says he'll hold it for me, so I don't have to lug it around all afternoon!"

Mindy glanced at the game booth clown, who nodded and said with a courteous smile, "Miss Alison, I can deliver it to your room if you like?"

We both nodded enthusiastically, giggling and sputtering out an almost incoherent but resounding, "Yes, please!" in between peals of laughter. Buoyed by the win, we skipped off toward the next booth, still riding the thrill of success.

This one was a maze, arranged like an enchanted candy bazaar, filled with peculiar bowls, ornate platters, mismatched cups, and, of course, grab bags. Since it was Halloween, every sweet—bonbons, mints, chews, caramels, toffees, chocolates—was sculpted into some kind of grotesque, festive shape. At the start of the line, we were each handed a personalized bowl—mine had my name scrawled across the inside in delicate bone-shaped lettering—so we could select one or two morsels per station.

Each treat was accompanied by a wickedly clever, darkly humorous description. We laughed over the absurdity of it all, hemming and hawing about whether to take one or two pieces, jostling elbows with other sugar-drunk revelers, comparing our loot as we went.

Once our bowls were brimming, we were ushered to a long table and served a warm, thick, cream-laced drink that could only be Bailey's Irish Cream—or some magical, ghostly variation. It was smooth, silky, and decadently rich. The perfect pairing. Each bite-sized treat had a distinct center—

nuts, liquors, caramels, colorful mousses—except one, a chocolate-covered nougat on a stick, disturbingly shaped like a slender bone.

Mindy, licking the gooey confection off before biting it in half, chuckled, "Nick really went all in with the theme this year. Every detail—everything—is disturbingly perfect. I mean, look at these cups! They could pass for carved-out hip bones. And those bowls? Definitely inverted skulls. Even the platters look like they're resting on real hands or perched atop severed necks."

I nodded, chewing thoughtfully. "I honestly can't believe the boys would skip this party for anything. At this point," I muttered, more to myself than to her, "I almost hope Danny doesn't come back. I'm having such a good time—and I don't even feel guilty about all this delicious, fattening madness without him."

"I don't know about you," I said after a moment, "but I need to get up and move."

"Agreed," Mindy said, grinning. "If I don't start walking it off, I'm going to be rolled to the parking lot tomorrow like a Halloween meatball."

We dove back into the carnival full-throttle. We played every game in sight—dart the balloon, water cannons, bottle ring toss, duck fishing. We hurled basketballs at hoops, pounded mallets to ring the bell, arm-wrestled a mechanical monster. We spun prize wheels, laughed off weight guessers, flirted with tarot cards, but drew the line when a silent stranger offered to paint our faces.

We indulged in everything edible: cotton candy, candy apples, apple fritters, fried Oreos, deep-fried cookie dough, cookie dough ice cream, fried cheesecake, fried cornbread, kettle corn, corn dogs, hot dogs—but firmly declined the fried pickles and tomatoes. Too healthy.

We rode everything: the Double Ferris Wheel, Hyperloop, Zipper, Swinger, Sky Wheel, Dodgem Cars, Bullet, Dragon Coaster, Rockin'

Starship, Looping Cages, Paratrooper, Giant Swings, Super Slide, and even the Merry-go-Round—twice.

In between all, we wandered through the funhouse again and again, just as Nick had encouraged, and each time it was wildly different—new paths, new illusions, new surprises around each bend. And then, on our final pass through, we emerged into twilight. The sun was setting, dinner was laid out in a glowing spectacle, and the musicians had just begun tuning up for the night's festivities.

I had never laughed so hard in my life.

How had I lived this long and never known such a light, giddy, weightless joy? I looked at Mindy—really looked—and realized I'd never had a friend quite like her. Someone who made me laugh so much I feared for my bladder. Someone who matched my absurdity, my energy, my wonder.

Now, seated for what felt like the hundredth time in one of the many pristine bathrooms set up for the carnival guests, I felt it hit me. A realization—not just that I hadn't seen Danny all day, but that... I didn't miss him. Not even a little. Not in that deep, aching way I always thought I should.

I glanced at the neatly stocked toilet paper roll and felt oddly complete.

As I exited the remarkably clean stall, I was greeted by a clown—tastefully eerie—offering me a towel to dry my hands. I accepted it, walked to the mirror, and paused. There I was: taller somehow, slimmer, glowing. Radiant. Happy.

And I knew in that instant—I wanted to bottle this day, this joy, this me, and keep it sealed forever.

Chapter 5

Finding a table, we filled our plates with a sampling of every dish in sight. There were three long tables, each overflowing with dozens of sides—no two alike. Not a single platter sat empty, and wherever my eyes landed, the food looked as though it had just come off the fire pit or out of the fridge. Juicy, glistening, slathered in sauce, bursting with color—meats, vegetables, cheeses, and fruits that looked freshly picked. Sauces both hot and chilled stood ready, none with a skin or film, and each time I glanced back, a clean spoon appeared in place. You'd never guess this was a standard barbecue buffet.

"Mindy, if this is a barbecue in Nevada, Lord, find me a house nearby!" Like most of the diners, we ate far more than we spoke. I might've spent the day grazing on candy and junk food—steadily paired with increasingly excellent mystery concoctions—but I was ravenous for real food.

I caught sight of Nick and waved him over. In between bites, I asked, "Did you ever find Danny or Alex? I haven't seen either of them, but I do see my car back in the lot over there."

For the briefest moment, a ripple of unease twisted in my stomach, but I pushed it aside and added, "Odd—it wasn't there earlier. But maybe I just missed it when we came out after lunch."

"No," Nick replied, "I haven't seen either of them. But I will tell you—and I feel a little strange even bringing this up—but at the Golden Lamp, a Chinese diner over in Mizpah, the waitress said she thought she recognized both Alex and Danny from my descriptions. They came in with a group of about ten people late last night—around eleven—for drinks and snacks."

He paused for a second, then continued, "The group was already pretty drunk, and when they left, they'd left a huge tip on the table—almost $500. The bill was only $135. Just 11 beers, 3 sodas, and 5 shareable appetizers. The waitress was thrilled, which is why she is pretty sure it was them."

Mindy leaned in, curious. "Did the waitress hear where they went next? Did anyone else see them afterward?"

Nick shook his head. "No. And Danny's car wasn't spotted either. The waitress said she didn't see how they arrived or how they left."

Just then, the music began to pick up, and someone called Nick's name from across the venue. He looked back at us. "I'm not sure what else I can do here, but I've got to go get this thing started. Let's talk more later if you'd like." With a small bow, he turned and made his way toward the stage.

Mindy and I exchanged glances, each of us caught in our own thoughts. I was thinking… Do I go to the dance? Should I drive to Mizpah myself? Call the police and report Danny missing? Could he have taken off with someone else? I didn't have the answers. Mindy had stood and was heading to a bistro table at the edge of the dance floor. I aimlessly trailed after her, confusion more than concern, tumbling over in my mind.

Drinks began flowing as the music swelled. We sipped slowly, letting the rhythm coax me out of my thoughts. After a while, we gave in to it all—the music, the mood, the mystery—and joined the crowd. And then we danced. Just danced.

Chapter 6
Homeward Bound

It felt like mere minutes had passed, but the sky was beginning to lighten. A small crowd remained in full swing, and the band still looked as fresh as if they were just kicking off the first set. Mindy and I had spent most of the night side by side, only parting to grab another round of drinks or snacks. But now, morning had arrived, and though we were both utterly spent, there was a buzz of exhilaration still humming in our bones. The rising sun seemed to jolt everyone into the realization that the Halloween Misfits party had lasted the night—and now, it was time to bring it to a close for another year.

Mindy stretched, her voice thick with fatigue. "Alison, I'm heading to my room. Going to catch a few hours of shut-eye. If Alex still isn't around by noon, I'm heading back to Winnemucca. He'll turn up eventually, I'm sure. And if not… well, that's just life sometimes. That's become my philosophy over the years."

She turned to go, then hesitated. Glancing back, she asked, "Alison, what are you going to do?"

I kept my gaze on the sunrise and said, "I guess I'll do the same and head back to Phoenix. It's hard to believe Danny would just disappear like this, but honestly… he didn't even want to come here. So maybe he left early—maybe I'll find him back home."

"For now, I think I'll stay and watch the full sunrise. Then I'll catch a few hours of sleep before I hit the road. I'll see you at checkout—noon, alright?" I said, turning my face once more toward the eastern sky.

Epilogue

The early fall snow had melted just enough for travelers to cross the Reno Pass and head south toward Vegas. A young couple in an open-top BMW was attempting—though not quite succeeding—to channel the spirit of Kerouac's On the Road as they came fishtailing into the dusty parking lot of the Clown Motel.

"Do you see that window display?" the man said, squinting toward the front of the building. "It looks like something straight out of a B-movie set in Hollywood!"

"Well, the guidebook said there were some interesting things here, and I want to check out the gift shop," the woman replied with a huff. "Even if you don't. Sit in the car if you think it's beneath you." With that, she stomped off into the motel and headed straight for the shop.

She wandered the aisles until something

caught her eye: a table near the back, displaying a dozen miniature stages. Each had its own troupe of animated clowns. She leaned in for a closer look. She had never seen anything quite like them.

Each stage came to life with clowns performing tiny acrobatic tricks—without strings, without visible magnets. The theme and music for each display were entirely distinct. One stage featured cheerful clowns riding minibikes and launching sparkles from a tiny cannon to the soundtrack of Barnum and Bailey circus music—an echo of a show that had long since shuttered. Another set of French Pierrot clowns, dressed in elegant black and white, evoked the streets of Paris with haunting, accordion-laced melodies.

But the one that truly mesmerized her played not only music, but also a background track of an audience—clapping, murmuring, and even tossing in the occasional whoop or cheer. The clowns wore traditional face makeup, but their costumes had a

Western flair—more cowboy than circus. Two clowns chased a bull across the stage, herding it into a pen. Moments later, a sheep emerged with a child riding its back. The sheep galloped in circles while a buzzer rang, prompting one clown to pluck the child from its woolly steed while the other corralled the animal through a chute. Just seconds later, the scene shifted to yet another cowboy skit.

She checked the price tag—steep, no doubt. But this was truly one-of-a-kind. Convinced she wouldn't find anything like it anywhere else, she flagged down the desk clerk and asked to have it boxed up.

The clerk arrived promptly and assured her they'd take care of the packaging while she continued to browse. After she paid, the clerk carried the carefully wrapped miniature stage to the convertible and placed it on the back seat as requested.

With the package secure, both the man and the woman ventured into the hotel's miniature room and museum. The displays proved unsettling enough to make them pass on lunch at the motel. Instead, they decided to head for the nearby town of Mizpah. The day was still young, and they had several more hours of road ahead before reaching their planned stop: Las Vegas.

The End

About The Author

A retired psychologist, cop, global business executive, and now hobbyist in stained glass, Fleming brings a unique blend of analytical depth and creative vision to her storytelling. She has traveled extensively around the world and those experiences inspire rich cultural textures and emotional insight into her work. She finds magic, tragedy, comedy, and in-your-gut unease everyday, transforming the ordinary into the extraordinary through her writing. Whether guiding readers through the landscapes of the mind or the streets of distant cities, her stories are shaped by a life of curiosity, imagination, and vibrant perspective.

www.ingramcontent.com/pod-product-compliance
Lightning Source LLC
Chambersburg PA
CBHW040834010826
48978CB00012BB/758